SCREAMS IN SPACE

Raintree is an imprint of Capstone Global Library Limited, a company incorporated in England and Wales having its registered office at 264 Banbury Road, Oxford, OX2 7DY – Registered company number: 6695582

www.raintree.co.uk
myorders@raintree.co.uk

Original illustrations © Capstone Global Library Limited 2020
Originated by Capstone Global Library Ltd
Printed and bound in India

ISBN 978 1 4747 7204 4
23 22 21 20 19
10 9 8 7 6 5 4 3 2 1

British Library Cataloguing in Publ
A full catalogue record for this book i

SCREAMS IN SPACE

ALIEN LOCKDOWN

BY AILYNN COLLINS
ILLUSTRATED BY JUAN CALLE

raintree

a Capstone company — publishers for children

INTO THE DARK...

When you look up at the night sky, do you ever wonder if scary, creepy, horrible things happen up there just as they do on Earth? Sounds can't travel through outer space because there's no air. So if frightened people were out there, we'd never even hear their screams . . .

In the not-too-distant future in *Alien Lockdown*, Yin and her classmates go on a field trip to an orbiting space station. The human scientists there are studying new alien life. Yin is excited, Sam is nervous and Priya isn't sure what to expect. But once they're aboard, all three friends will feel the exact same thing — terror!

1

The room was packed. People were standing in long queues for tickets. Groups of tourists huddled together as they waited for their guides to lead the way to the space pods.

Yin Nova and her classmates, wearing matching school uniforms, sat against a wall. They watched returning passengers step out from the launch bays. Yin's legs couldn't stop bouncing up and down. She had been dreaming of this day for a long time.

Her friend Sam was less excited. "You know it's Friday the thirteenth today, right?" Sam moaned. "It's the unluckiest day of the year. And not a good day for a class field trip to space."

Yin laughed. Her best friend could find the negative in any situation. "Lighten up, Sam!"

"Yeah, you know that's just a silly belief," said Priya, the third in their best friend trio.

"I know what will get you excited," Yin said, pulling Sam to her feet. Priya followed behind.

Yin led her friends to a display of giant photos on the opposite wall. When the three came to a stop, the photos began to shimmer and grow. The images turned into 3-D holograms.

Yin pointed to one. "Look at it. International Space Station Three," she said. The station was built like a long stick with seven rings balancing along its length.

"The ISS 3 is bigger than the two older space stations put together," Yin continued. "And today, we get to go aboard the real thing."

"Yeah, the museum we're going to is right here," Priya added. She pointed to the third ring. "It has the largest collection of space artefacts in the world."

"You mean space junk," Sam said, frowning. "They just collect the stuff our ancestors threw away in space and call it artefacts."

"Maybe. But we don't care about *that*," Yin said. She touched the hologram and focused in on one room in the museum. "*This* is what we are going to space for."

The girls stared at the hologram. The room Yin had pointed out held the most exciting exhibit. It had been the talk of people on Earth for the past year.

"The first alien plant life ever found," Yin whispered in awe. "Do you know what this means?"

Sam crossed her arms. "That it'll turn into a monster and eat us all, ending life on Earth?"

"No, Sam," Priya said, patting her friend on the back. "Scientists studied the plant before they opened the exhibit. It's perfectly safe."

Yin stared at the tiny image of the glass cabinet that held the plant. "Just think. A team of astronauts was exploring a large rock in space. They think it broke off from an actual planet far out there somewhere."

"And on that rock," Priya continued, "they found this plant – *Lilidae Spatium Efloupos*. Otherwise known as the Star Cabbage."

"That's a stupid name," Sam muttered.

Yin's eyes widened with wonder. "Finding the plant means there could be another world where humans can live."

"Oh, so now that we've ruined our home, we can just give up on Earth and ruin another planet?" Sam said.

"Wow, Sam, that's a terrible thing to say," Yin said. "How can you—"

Yin was going to keep arguing, but their teacher, Mr Olu, whistled to get the class' attention. All twelve of his class returned to the wall. In his hands, the teacher held a box.

"As a special treat," Mr Olu said, grinning, "the gift shop has given us free ice lollies."

The kids cheered as Mr Olu handed out the frozen snacks. The ice lollies were shaped like a space pod. Each one was a long tube with pointed ends.

"It just looks like a colourful egg to me," Sam said. She didn't take one for herself.

Yin and Priya were too busy eating to reply, but they both gave her their best glares. Trust Sam to put down everything fun.

Sam sighed. "You know, I'm not the only one who isn't excited about this alien thing."

She tapped the sleeve of her uniform jacket. A hologram in the shape of a screen popped out of her right arm. It was her Holo computer coming to life. The Holo played a video of a crowd protesting in a city square. A young woman with dark, curly hair was speaking angrily from a stage at the front.

"See," Sam said. She shoved the Holo screen in front of her friends' noses. "This is a group called Earth First. They've been trying to get the ISS 3 to return the alien object—"

"Plant!" Yin interrupted.

"Whatever. Earth First says the Star Cabbage is dangerous. We don't know anything about where it came from," Sam said. Her eyes narrowed. "Earth First believes we should stop wasting money looking for other planets to live on. We should focus on making our own planet better. It's our home. We shouldn't just dump it because we've done a bad job taking care of it."

"Whoa, that's the most you've ever said in one breath, Sam," Yin said. Priya giggled next to her.

Sam pulled her arm away, and the Holo screen disappeared. "You two never take me seriously," she mumbled. "I give up."

"Good," Yin said, licking the last drops of melted ice lolly off her fingers. "Now you can focus on enjoying our first and only field trip into space."

"Listen, everyone," Mr Olu said.

The teacher had appeared in front of the class again. This time a younger man stood by his side. The young man waved to the class.

"This is Brome, our pod pilot," Mr Olu said. "He'll take us up to the station and hand us over to the museum guide. Then he'll bring us back down when we're finished."

Brome smilcd and rubbed his hands together. "There are five pods that go up to the ISS 3. Each one is attached to a special, super-long nano-tube cable," he explained. "Remember, the pods have to travel all the way through Earth's atmosphere and into space, so the cable has to be really strong."

Brome pauscd and looked at the class. "Any questions so far?"

"I have one," Sam said. "How much money has been wasted on these space pods?"

Brome just gave Sam a tight smile and went on to talk about the history of the pods. Yin noticed Mr Olu pull out a napkin and press it to his mouth. His skin went from brown to grey, and his eyes became watery.

"Are you OK, Mr Olu?" Yin asked.

Brome stopped talking, and everyone's eyes went to the teacher. Mr Olu started to reply, but he quickly covered his mouth again. He turned away and rushed straight for the toilets. Brome ran after him. The class let out a collective groan.

Yin couldn't believe it. Friday the thirteenth really was a bad luck day.

Everyone in the class started talking at the same time.

"We were so close!" Mike said.

"It's probably just nerves," Priya added.

"Maybe Mr O had a bad ice lolly?" Ian said.

Yin was so disappointed she couldn't even speak. It didn't matter why Mr Olu was sick. The class wouldn't be able to visit the ISS 3 if their teacher wasn't feeling well.

"It's a sign," Sam said. "Like I said, it's not a good day for space travel."

Brome returned to where the kids were sitting. He looked a bit sick too.

"It seems your teacher ate or drank something that's made him very ill," Brome said. "I'm sorry, but you'll have to miss today's trip. I'll put you all on the waiting list for the next opportunity."

Yin groaned. Around her, the rest of the class protested loudly.

"But it could take forever to get tickets again!" Mike shouted. "We probably won't even be in Mr Olu's class by then!"

Yin jumped to her feet. She had spent the whole year learning about the pods, the ISS 3 and the Star Cabbage. She was too close to give up now.

"What if *you* take us, Brome?" she said.
"It's just one trip straight up to the ISS 3, and
you'll hand us over to the museum guide, right?
It's not like the pods can get lost on the way."

Brome laughed, but Yin noticed beads of sweat
forming on his forehead.

"We promise to be the best-behaved customers
you've ever had," Yin said. She looked around
at her classmates. They all sat up straighter and
nodded their heads. "Please?" Yin added.

Brome gulped. He couldn't refuse them. So
he went off to "ask the authorities", as he put it.
Twenty minutes later, he returned.

"All right, I will take you up," Brome said.
He looked terrified. "You must all swear that you'll
do exactly as I say, or we'll just turn around and
come straight back."

As the class cheered, Yin leaned over to her friends. "He can't turn the pods around," she said. "The pods go up one at a time along the cable. There's no turning back, no matter what."

"Now I'm not feeling so well," Sam said.

"Too late," Yin said. She pulled Sam into the line with her. "We're going up!"

Yin's mouth dropped open as she stared at the space pod. It was a tall, silver tube that narrowed to a point at the top and bottom. It reminded Yin of a jet plane standing on its end. Each of its four levels had a large window that went almost all the way around the pod. Through the windows, Yin could see rows of yellow seats.

"I don't want a window seat," Sam said, twirling a strand of blonde hair tightly around her finger. "I get motion sickness."

"All seats face a window," Yin said. Next to her, Sam whimpered. "Just keep your eyes shut. I'll tell you when there's something good to look at."

Brome led the class up a tall set of metal stairs by the side of the pod. At the very top of the huge tube, he pushed open a door. "You have this pod to yourselves today. Aren't you all lucky?"

Inside the pod, the kids followed a smaller spiral staircase down to the middle two levels. They held the passenger seats. The three friends sat down in the wide, comfy yellow seats on the second level.

"Strap yourselves in." Brome's voice boomed over the speakers.

Something rumbled behind Yin's head, and seat belts appeared at her shoulders. She pulled the straps down and clicked them into place. Sam and Priya did the same.

Yin's heart raced. This was really happening. She was going into space.

"Welcome to the space pod *Discovery*," Brome announced. "The *Discovery* is the smallest of all the pods and, in my opinion, the cosiest. Our trip to the ISS 3 will take six hours."

"That's not so long," Priya whispered to Sam. "It'll be fun."

Sam groaned.

Brome continued. "The space pod rises fifty thousand kilometres above Earth, or thirty-one thousand miles. There are actually three stations attached to the cable. The ISS 3 is the lowest one, at two thousand kilometres. Our pod only goes to the ISS 3, though, so don't ask me to take you any higher."

Brome laughed. It sounded rehearsed.

"The ride might get bumpy as we rise through Earth's atmosphere," Brome said. "But once we're in outer space, it'll be completely smooth. Artificial gravity will make it seem as if you never left Earth. You'll be free to walk around the pod and get lunch on the lowest level."

Brome went on, but no one was listening any more. Excited chatter filled Yin's level.

Until there was a loud thud, and the pod jerked upwards. Everyone fell silent. Yin noticed Sam was gripping her seat belts.

"Nothing to worry about," Brome announced. "We're just leaving the station. If you feel sick, there are bags in the seat pockets. Please remember to seal them tightly when you've . . . uh . . . finished. We don't want any spillage!"

"I'm feeling sick already," Sam moaned. She grabbed the bag and placed it over her mouth.

"Here we go," Brome said. "Next stop, International Space Station Three!"

The kids whooped as the pod began to rise. Everything rattled. Yin felt the weight of her body press downwards into her feet.

"Think of this as the beginning of a roller coaster ride," Yin said, giving Sam's hand a squeeze. "You love those."

Sam moaned again and shut her eyes.

"Outer space, here we come!" Priya squealed.

As they travelled higher, Yin tried to point out the scenery to Sam, but she refused to open her eyes. Priya leaned forward as much as she could against the seat belt straps. She and Yin gasped at the ever-shrinking ocean below them. For about ten minutes the pod shook like a plane flying through a storm. Sam threw up but remembered to seal the bag tight.

"We're about to leave the atmosphere," Brome said. "Ready for the experience of a lifetime?"

Yin could hear both levels clap and shout. Her own cheer was the loudest.

Brome began the countdown. "Three . . . two . . . one!"

The pod gave one last massive shudder. Then there was silence.

For a moment Yin thought Brome had turned off the engines. There was no more humming and no more rattling. Nothing. She felt as if she was floating on a cloud.

"Look out of your windows," Brome said.

Yin gasped. Even Sam opened her eyes. Through the thick glass, they could spot a few stars in the distance, but space was mostly black nothingness for as far as they could see.

Below them was Earth. It seemed to glow in the blackness, lit up by the Sun overhead. Swirls of white clouds covered the blue and brown world like a blanket. None of the holograms Yin had studied prepared her for seeing her planet with her own eyes.

Yin couldn't look away. She thought about how with each second, she was moving further away from her family, her teacher and the other billions of people on Earth. She didn't have the safety of the ground beneath her feet any more.

She was in outer space, the most exciting place she could imagine. But it was also the most dangerous. Sam's words about Friday the thirteenth came back to her mind.

A shiver ran down Yin's back. Whatever happened next, it was too late to turn back.

3

It wasn't the sudden jerk that woke Yin up. It was Sam's sharp whisper.

"We're here." Sam's fingernails dug deep into Yin's hand.

"Ow! Lighten up, Sam," Yin said, blinking over at her friend. Somewhere in the six-hour journey, she had fallen asleep. Now she was wide awake.

"Welcome to ISS 3!" Brome called through the speakers. "We've just docked. Please wait in your seats while I open the docking doors."

"See? That wasn't so bad," Yin said to Sam.

Sam shook her head. "The ride was just the—"

A loud thud interrupted her. Then all the lights went out. Yin felt Sam's hands grab her again as the pod filled with screams.

"What's going on?" Sam cried.

The lights flickered back on, but they were red this time. The dim light made it look as if everything was covered in blood.

"Those are emergency lights," Priya whispered.

Yin felt like she might need the sick bag. "So what's the emergency?" she asked.

The loudspeakers crackled. Brome was trying to say something, but only a few words could be heard. Finally, Brome himself walked down onto their level.

"Please stay calm, everyone," he said. "We've just run into a small problem. I can't reach anyone on the station."

Sam began to cry. Other kids were crying too. Yin bit her upper lip and breathed slowly through her nose. She wasn't going to freak out.

The sound system crackled again, but it couldn't be from Brome. He was standing right in front of them.

"The ISS 3 is on lockdown," a robotic voice said loudly. The class stopped crying to listen. "Please head to your secure station and await instructions. This is not a drill. The ISS 3 is on lockdown."

"What does that mean?" Sam asked.

Before Brome could answer, the kids who were sitting on the level below came up the stairs behind him. Everyone was talking at once. Most kids were asking Brome if they could go home.

"Quiet!" Brome raised his hands as if in surrender. "Let me explain! The station can go on lockdown for any number of reasons," he said. "It means something needs fixing, and they need everyone to stay in their rooms while the fixing happens. That's all."

A few kids sighed in relief.

"Besides, the base on Earth would've been notified," Brome continued. "If the problem is serious, they'll send help. Give me a few minutes so I can try to contact someone. Then we'll have a better picture of what's going on. OK?"

The class mumbled their agreement, and Brome left the kids to themselves.

"I'm calling my mum," Sam said, sticking out her sleeve. Her Holo screen popped up, but it just crackled with static. Sam blinked back more tears. "Th-there's no connection."

Priya tried her Holo. The same fuzz filled her screen. "Are we too far from Earth?" she asked.

"I don't think so," Yin said. "The ISS 3 speaks with Earth all the time. The lockdown is probably a problem with their communication systems."

A few minutes later, Brome came back. The kids all looked up, hoping for good news.

"I wasn't able to reach anyone. It appears the ISS 3 is having some power issues. But I've found the wheel that opens the station door," Brome said, looking pleased. "I'll need some help with it."

Yin was the first to volunteer. Priya and some of the boys did the same. Sam stayed firmly planted in her seat. The kids followed Brome, climbing the stairs to the top level.

When they arrived at the docking point, Yin saw that their pod's doors were already open. A short bridge linked them to the ISS 3.

On the other end of the bridge stood a door with a flashing red light at the top. To the right was a large blue wheel. Brome put his hands on it.

"Usually, the station door opens on its own when a pod docks," he said. "With the lockdown, the only way to open it is by turning this wheel. I'll warn you, it's pretty stiff."

On Brome's count, they turned the wheel with all their might. It was hard work. The wheel turned a few centimetres at a time. It took several minutes before the door opened just wide enough to let a person through.

"Finally!" Yin cried, rubbing her sore hands together. "Now we can get someone to help us." She rushed towards the door.

"Wait," Brome said. He held up a hand to stop Yin. "You should wait here while I get help. You kids aren't as familiar with the station as I am."

Yin wrinkled her nose. She didn't like Brome's idea, but she couldn't argue. After all, they had promised to be his best-behaved customers.

But that was before everything went wrong, she thought.

The robot voice came on again. "The ISS 3 is on lockdown. Please head to your secure station and await instructions. This is not a drill."

Brome rubbed his eyebrow. "I'll be back as soon as I can." He squeezed through the tight gap in the door and disappeared.

Priya, the boys and Yin returned to their classmates on the second level. The kids all sat together as they waited, and they just stared out of the window into space. No one felt like talking any more.

"What if it's that Star Cabbage plant?" Sam said suddenly. Her voice made everyone jump. "Brome has been gone for so long. What if the plant ate him and it's coming for us next? They should've called it Monster Cabbage!"

A few kids gasped. Sam was squeezing a blob of pink putty in her hands. She always carried a ball of it in her pocket. It helped her calm down when she was nervous.

"Don't be ridiculous!" Yin snapped. "You're just scaring people."

Sam began to sob quietly.

Yin immediately felt awful. "I'm sorry, Sam."

A thought came to her, though. What if Sam was right? Not about the Star Cabbage. Yin knew that was impossible. But what if something had happened to Brome and he couldn't help them? It had been a while since he'd left.

Yin got to her feet and wiped her sweaty hands on her uniform trousers. "You're right. Brome has been away for too long. We should do something."

"Like what?" Priya asked. She blinked tears out of her eyes.

"The announcement said that station staff should go to secure rooms. There must be some on the level we're docked to," Yin said. She felt braver as her idea began to take shape in her mind. "We should find one of those rooms and get help."

The classmates looked at each other. No one moved. Yin huffed.

"Well, I'm going," she said. "I can't just sit around and wait for something to happen."

Without another word, Yin turned and headed for the docking door.

"Wait for us!" Sam cried.

Yin stopped in surprise just as she was about to squeeze through the space station door. She hadn't expected any of her classmates to follow her, and Sam least of all.

"I'm not staying here if you're not," Sam said. She was still holding her putty, but her face was determined.

"Me too," Priya said. "I'm worried something happened to Brome."

Behind her, Mike, Ian and Sung stood nodding their heads.

Yin exhaled. She was glad she didn't have to go alone.

"OK, good. So here's the plan," she said. "Let's split into two teams. The ISS 3 is made up of seven levels of rings. They're all attached in the middle to a long rod called the central core. We should be on the lowest level, the smallest ring, so it shouldn't take long to walk around it."

The others nodded. They'd all studied the station in class. This was not new information.

"Sam, Priya and I will go out to the left. You boys go right," Yin said. "Knock on every door until someone answers. If we don't find anything, we should meet on the other side of the ring."

Sam shivered. "What if we get lost?"

Yin tried not to roll her eyes. How could they get lost if each level was just one big circle?

"Do you have your putty?" Yin asked.

"Yeah," Sam said. She held out the bright pink blob. "Why?"

"If you're so worried, stick pieces of the putty onto the wall as we walk," Yin explained. "We can follow them back to the pod."

Everyone agreed on the plan. One by one, the kids squeezed through the door.

The ISS 3 was bigger than Yin had imagined. To the left and right, the corridor stretched on for what seemed like forever. Yin knew this level was a ring, but the corridor didn't seem to curve. It looked straight.

This place is gigantic! Yin thought.

Blue emergency lights pulsed slowly overhead. A damp smell filled the air, which was odd because nothing but white metal panels lined the corridor. The lights and smell made Yin feel dizzy.

But it was the thick silence that was the worst. It felt as if someone had stuffed cotton into Yin's ears. It hurt.

Without another word, the boys went right. The girls turned left. Sam stopped every twenty steps and stuck a piece of putty onto the wall.

Soon the girls came across a computer panel. Yin touched the screen, hoping to get information. The screen stayed black. They moved on.

"There's a door," Priya said, pointing ahead on their right.

They ran up to it. They knocked so hard their fists ached.

"Help! Please help us!" the girls called out together.

No one answered. The only sound in the corridor was their own breathing.

The girls tried the next door. And the next. After the third door, there was a long corridor to their right.

"That must lead to the central core," Yin said, remembering holograms of the station's structure. Down the corridor she could see more doors and other corridors. "That would take us to the station's main lift to get to other levels."

They kept walking and knocking on doors. But there were no signs of life.

Yin couldn't even spot any clues as to why the station was on lockdown. Nothing looked out of place. It was as if the station crew had just disappeared.

"Maybe there aren't secure rooms on this level," Priya said finally. "Should we try another one?"

Yin shook her head. "No, let's wait until we meet up with the boys."

But as they continued on, Yin wondered why they hadn't run into the boys yet. They'd been walking for a while. Secretly, she was glad Sam was sticking putty on the walls. If they walked all the way around this level, at least they would see the putty pieces.

"What's that?" Sam shrieked suddenly.

The girls all froze. "What is what?" Priya whispered.

"There!" Sam said, pointing to their right.

A shadow crossed the end of the corridor. It was fast and big. Big enough that it might've been Brome or another station staff member.

"Hey!" Yin called out. "We need help!"

"*Shhh!*" Priya said, grabbing Yin's arm tightly. "We don't know what it is."

Yin scowled at her. "Don't tell me Sam has got you imagining monsters too? That could be someone who'll help us!"

She pulled away from her friend and ran after the shadow. It flickered again at the end of the corridor. It was heading the other way now.

Yin took off after the shadow, running as fast as she could. But the shadow was faster. She followed it down one corridor, then through a side corridor. She turned into another corridor, and another. She heard her friends trying to keep up behind her.

Yin finally stopped, panting. They were in a long, empty corridor. There was no sign of the shadow.

"If that was a person, why didn't they stop for us?" Priya wondered aloud.

"Maybe it was just a station drone, sent out to make repairs during the lockdown?" Yin said through heavy breaths. She was a good runner, and yet that shadow had always been out of reach.

"Um, where are we?" Sam asked, looking around. "Which way did we come?"

"I don't know!" Yin snapped.

The white corridors all looked the same. And the blue lights flashing overhead were making it hard to think. Yin was getting tired of this adventure. She took a deep breath and let it out slowly.

"We haven't left the first level, so we should be able to find our way back," Yin said. "Look for your putty, Sam."

They searched along the walls in silence for a long time. No one wanted to be the first to say what was obvious – and what they feared.

Finally, Sam spoke up.

"Guys?" she said. Her voice was shaky. "My putty. It's gone."

5

"How can the putty be gone?" Yin said. She looked around the corridor. There was no sign of the boys, the shadow or the pieces of putty.

"Maybe the pieces fell off?" Priya said.

"Then they should be on the floor!" Sam gripped the tiny blob she still had left. "Besides, I stuck them on really hard. What's going on?"

Yin didn't answer straight away. She couldn't stop panting, and her insides felt like jelly.

But it had been her idea to leave the pod. She had to keep a cool head. So, Yin swallowed her fear.

"We must've gone onto the second level somehow," Yin said. "It's the only explanation."

"That doesn't make sense!" Priya said. "How did we get onto a different level if we didn't take any stairs or get in the lift?"

Yin huffed. "Maybe the levels change with ramps, and we were too busy running after that . . . whatever it was . . . to notice?"

"You mean *you* were busy running after it," Priya snapped. "We were following you just so we didn't get split up."

"I knew we should've waited for Brome," Sam said, twisting the bit of putty in her hands. "Why did you make us come out here, Yin?"

Yin squeezed her fingernails into her palms. "I didn't make—" she began.

A low rumble echoed down the corridor. Everything Yin wanted to say suddenly vanished from her brain.

"What was that?" Sam whispered.

"It's probably one of the station's systems powering back on," Yin said. But she was whispering too.

Yin began to walk forward – fast. The other two girls followed close behind.

"Guys . . . wait!" Priya said. She had stopped and was pointing to something.

It was a door with a hole punched through its middle. Jagged bits of material twisted outwards. It was like an open mouth with hundreds of sharp teeth, ready to swallow the girls in one bite.

"What can bust through a door like that?" Priya asked.

"The same thing that made that noise earlier," Sam whispered. "An alien monster. It must've caused the lockdown."

Yin crossed her arms to stop them shaking. "Whatever it is, it's not here any more," she said. "The hole is bent outwards. Something escaped from inside."

"We shouldn't be wandering around if something is on the loose. We have to go back to the pod," Priya said. She and Sam started to walk away.

Yin moved closer to the door. "If something escaped from here, maybe it's the safest place to hide. It won't come back, right?" She didn't know if she was making sense, but she was tired and needed a moment to think.

"We don't even know where we are," Yin argued. "I say we take a break and work it out."

She stepped through the hole.

"Are you crazy?" Sam said from outside.

Priya called, "Come back, Yin!"

But Yin ignored them. Carefully, she looked around the room.

It was a lab. White workbenches filled the room in neat rows. On top of them lay complicated-looking scientific equipment. A few chairs were knocked over, but other than that, everything seemed pretty normal.

Then, something at the back caught Yin's attention.

"Guys, look at this," Yin said, heading further inside. Sam and Priya slowly came into the lab.

On the back workbench were several plants. Bunches of long, thick stems rose out of large pots. Only the stems weren't green – they were beige and light brown. It made the stems look more like chubby, handless arms. At the end of those arms grew thin vines that curled out like tiny snakes reaching for their prey.

"It's the Star Cabbage," Yin whispered. This was the thing she'd come all the way into space to see. She'd nearly forgotten about it during the chaos of the lockdown.

She smiled. The vines seemed to stretch towards her, as if they were happy to see her too.

Impossible, thought Yin. Still, a shiver ran through her – excitement and nervousness mixed together. She reached for one of the plants.

"What are you doing?" Sam said, grabbing Yin's hand. "That could be a monster!"

"Don't be silly," Yin said. She pulled away. "It's a plant. How could it break through a solid metal door?"

"Well, don't touch it anyway," Priya added. "Just in case."

But Yin knew it was harmless. As her friends turned away to search the lab, she couldn't help herself. Yin reached out again.

The plant was cool and smooth. But when she stroked it, tiny red hairs began to grow all over the plant. One of the thin vines curled around her finger, gently. It tickled.

"Over here!" Priya called. She was pointing to the floor on the other side of the lab. "I've found something."

Yin turned, but the plant wouldn't let go of her finger. She tugged her hand away, and the vine broke off the plant.

Oops! Yin glanced over at her friends to see if they'd noticed. They were busy looking at what Priya had found. She peeled the vine off her finger. She bit back a gasp as its tiny hairs scratched her. Then she stuck the plant piece into her pocket.

Yin joined her friends, rubbing the itchy skin of her finger. "What is it?" she asked.

"Oh, it's just a shoe," Priya said, letting out a relieved sigh.

"Why would a shoe be lying around a lab? And what's that liquid around it?" Sam said.

Yin walked over to investigate. The liquid pooled around the shoe was thick and dark, almost black. She crouched down. As she got closer, she saw in the dim emergency lighting that the liquid wasn't black. It was red.

"That's blood!" Yin shouted, jumping back.

"B-blood?" Sam stammered.

Yin's stomach was queasy. "I think there's something else – inside the shoe," she said.

The girls looked at each other. They didn't need to check the shoe to know what was stuck inside, bleeding.

They all dashed to the door. Sam scrambled out first, followed by Priya. Yin had one leg out the door when a metallic screech echoed in the lab behind them.

Yin froze, even though she knew she should keep going. She should run from whatever had made that noise – and whatever had eaten the owner of the foot. But her body wouldn't obey her brain.

Before she could move another step, something brushed up against the back of her leg. Then it grabbed her.

6

Yin screamed.

Priya tugged on Yin's jacket. "Get out, quick!"

"NO!" a voice said.

Without thinking, Yin turned around. There was a human hand wrapped around her ankle. And attached to that hand was a woman in a white lab coat.

"It's not safe out there," the woman said. She let go of Yin and scrambled to her feet.

Priya and Sam stepped back inside to help Yin up. They huddled together by the door and stared at the woman who had appeared out of nowhere. Yin thought the woman looked familiar, but she couldn't remember where she'd seen her before.

"I apologize for scaring you," the woman said. She brushed a strand of curly black hair away from her dark eyes. "But you have to stay inside."

"Where did *you* come from?" Yin asked.

The woman pointed to an open panel on the wall by the door. It was a small cupboard. She must have been hiding in there all along.

"Now get away from the door!" The woman spoke roughly but quietly.

The girls hurried further inside the lab. They watched as the woman checked the ceiling, and then under the lab workbenches.

"What are you looking for?" Sam whispered.

The woman exhaled. "Nothing. Never mind." She waved towards the plants. "Just stay away from those, will you? Can't be too sure . . ." She mumbled something else that the girls couldn't catch. "Are you kids tourists? Why aren't you in your secure stations?"

"We're not tourists. We need help," Yin said. She told the woman what had happened to them.

The woman gasped. "Oh, I completely forgot about your class! I'm Calathea, the museum guide. The lockdown happened as I was on my way to meet you all at the docking bay. I had to duck into this lab, but . . ." Her hands began to shake. She pressed them together. "It was awful."

Yin wanted to ask what had been so awful, but another low rumble came from outside. This time, though, the rumble went on longer. It grew louder.

It sounded like an angry growl.

"It's found us!" Calathea cried.

She bolted back towards her hiding place. The girls ran after her, but Calathea put a hand out to stop them.

"No, there's not enough room! It's only a supply cupboard," she said. "You can hide under the workbenches."

Another deep roar made them all scream.

"That won't do any good!" Yin said.

"You have to help us!" Priya said.

"I'm sorry, but there's nothing I can do," Calathea said. "I–I'm new here. This is only my first week on the station."

Yin was getting impatient. "Where's the rest of the station crew then?"

"Most of them would be in the canteen, on the other side of this level." Calathea frowned. She was about to say more, but a third growl slashed through the air. This one was louder and closer. They were running out of time.

Yin's heart was racing, but her brain was working hard too. Before this trip, she had spent countless evenings studying the space station's layout. She forced herself to remember every hologram she'd seen. She looked up at the ceiling.

"Air vent tunnels run all through the station," Yin said.

"Air vents?" Calathea muttered.

Yin ignored her and continued. "The vents connect to every room. We can use one to get to the canteen without going through the corridors."

Calathea was already half crouched inside her cupboard. "Ha! Good luck with that."

"It's a great idea, Yin," Priya said. "How do we find one?"

Yin searched the ceiling. "There should be a – there!" she shouted. She pointed to a grate on the ceiling at the back of the lab.

"It's right above the monster plants!" Sam cried. "Calathea said not to go near them."

"If they're not hungry, you might have a chance," Calathea said. "Just don't make them angry." With that, she pulled the door shut. It creaked loudly.

But another sound made Yin's heart stop. A shuffling, scratching sound was coming from the corridor outside.

Yin and Priya dashed across the room to the workbench of plants. But Sam stood against the wall by Calathea's cupboard.

"No! Those Monster Cabbages could eat me!" Sam said.

"They're just plants," Yin hissed. "They don't eat people. Don't listen to Calathea."

She couldn't tell her friend that she had a piece of the plant in her pocket. And that, somehow, she knew they wouldn't hurt them. She rubbed her fingers. They still itched, but inside, Yin felt a peace she couldn't explain.

Yin turned towards the plants and gently moved a pot. Nothing happened. She smiled and climbed onto the bench. Luckily, the ceiling grate was within reach. She pulled, and it fell away.

"See, Sam? It's totally safe," Yin said. "Climb up and I'll help you get inside the vent."

Sam didn't move for a second. Then she hurried over, eyeing the plants. "I don't like this," she said as she put her foot in Yin's clasped hands.

"I don't like that it's so quiet," Priya whispered. "From what I know about predators, when they stop growling, they start pouncing."

Sam made a sound that was scarier to Yin than the growling. It gave Yin the strength to shove Sam up into the vent.

"Start crawling, Sam," Yin said. "We'll be right behind you."

Yin pushed Priya up next as Sam disappeared into the metal tunnel.

"Someone has to close the vent after we're inside," Priya called down to Yin. "Otherwise the creature could follow us."

Yin turned towards the closed wall cupboard. "Calathea!" she whispered. "If you won't come with us, at least help by putting the vent cover back on. OK?"

Calathea opened the panel just enough to stick her head out. "I'm not going anywhere near those plants," she said, her voice shaking. "You're on your own." She slammed the panel shut.

Yin wasn't about to waste time arguing. She gripped the edge of the vent, and Priya pulled her in the rest of the way.

The air vent tunnel was so small that Yin had to crawl on her hands and knees. She moved as fast as she could on the cold, slippery surface. The girls crawled forward, trying to put distance between them and the lab.

Then suddenly the metal walls of the tunnel shook. A snarl echoed down the vent, followed by a woman's horrific shriek.

7

"Calathea! It got Calathea!" Sam cried. She stopped and curled up her knees. "I can't do this any more. I want to go home."

"Keep moving!" Yin ordered. She could hear the anger in her voice, but she was too scared to hide it. "Get it together, Sam. We can't just sit here and wait to be eaten."

That made Sam cry even louder.

"*Shhh!*" Yin said. "The creature will hear you!"

"Give her a moment, Yin," Priya snapped. "She's tired and scared. We all are!"

"I'm just trying to keep us out of danger," Yin said.

"So *I'm* the one putting us in danger?" Sam said, sounding more and more angry. "Calathea is probably dead. And the monster is coming for us next. None of that is my fault."

"I didn't say it was your fault," Yin argued. "I just said–"

"Enough!" Priya interrupted. "This isn't the time to be fighting."

Yin sighed, frustrated. "That's why I said we have to keep moving!" But her friend wasn't budging, and the tunnel was too narrow to crawl around. "We're so close to the canteen, and to help. Go, Sam!"

"You know what?" Sam said, glaring at Yin. Her face was all red, just like her watery eyes. "No! Who made you the boss?"

Yin stared at her. "What?"

Sam lowered her head. Strands of her hair fell over her face like a curtain.

"This whole trip was your idea," Sam said. "I wanted to go camping at the zoo, like all the other classes in our year. You *had* to suggest going into space. And then you made us disobey Brome and go on this stupid mission. You are the bossiest person I've ever met."

Her words were like a punch to Yin's gut. Yin looked at Priya, who was examining her shoes with a lot of interest.

"Priya," Yin whispered, "do you think I'm bossy too?"

"I suppose," Priya said quietly. She looked straight up at Yin. "The truth is, sometimes, I feel like all you care about is what you want. You don't ever stop to ask what *we're* thinking." She wiped her forehead. "We really should keep moving."

"Oh, it's OK for *you* to give orders," Yin said. Her stomach hurt, and now her knees and hands were throbbing. "That's exactly what I said a second ago."

Her friends were silent.

"Whatever," Yin huffed. "That thing is still out there. Let's go."

"Fine!" Sam barked. She got back onto her hands and knees and headed forward.

Something in Yin's chest burned like a hot coal as she followed her friends. She would have lots to say when they got home. If they ever got home.

The tunnel ahead seemed to go on and on. And in the dim light, Yin felt as if the walls were closing in on them.

A drop of sweat fell from Yin's forehead onto her hand, right where the Star Cabbage had scratched her. Her skin stung. It was almost a nice distraction from her friends' mean words. She wondered, though, if maybe they were right about her.

Yin was so caught up in her thoughts that she fell behind the others. She sped up and just reached Priya when Sam stopped. They were at a T-junction in the tunnels.

"Left or right, Yin?" Sam sounded annoyed.

"Left," Yin said. At least, she was pretty sure that was the direction to the central core and the canteen.

But Sam didn't move. She tilted her head.

"I think I hear voices over here," Sam said. She began crawling down the right-hand tunnel.

"Wait," Yin called. "It doesn't make sense for the canteen to be that way."

"Maybe for once, you don't know everything," Sam told her. "You weren't the only one who studied the ISS 3. We *all* did." She kept going forward.

Priya sat at the junction. She wasn't sure who she should follow.

Yin wiped her sweaty forehead. It was getting hard to breathe in the tight tunnel. She didn't want to argue again, but they didn't have time for this.

"Come on, Sam," she called.

"No," Sam said. "I can hear something."

Yin shut her eyes and listened. At first, all she heard was her own heavy breathing and Priya's foot tapping against the wall of the tunnel.

Suddenly, there it was. A shuffling sound, like something sliding along the smooth tunnel surface. Then a low snort and the screech of sharp nails clawing deep into metal.

It was coming from the right.

"Sam—" Yin began to yell.

But it was too late. All she heard was the scraping of metal, and then a long, shrill scream.

8

Yin hesitated for what felt like the longest second in her life. Then she squeezed past Priya, heading in Sam's direction. She couldn't leave her friend to fight the monster alone. Up ahead a bright light shone. Had the monster clawed a hole into the tunnel?

"Sam!" Yin and Priya called at the same time.

As Yin got closer, she saw there was a hole in the floor, but it was a perfect square. It was an air vent grate, like the one they had used to get into the tunnels. Sam was nowhere to be seen.

Yin slowed. Strange sounds were coming up from the hole. She paused, trying to make out the noises above the pounding of her own heart.

She heard clapping. And laughter. And people talking!

She stuck her head through the hole and blinked at the bright light below.

"Yin! Priya! We're saved!" Sam's voice echoed up into the tunnel.

Yin's eyes got used to the light. She saw Sam standing in a large room filled with tables and chairs – and lots of people. Some were dressed in ISS 3 uniforms, and others wore ordinary clothes. They'd found the canteen!

"Why did you scream, Sam?" Yin called.

"Yeah," Priya said, squeezing next to Yin. "You scared us to death!"

Sam grinned. "Sorry. After I took off the grate, I fell through the hole. Luckily some people caught me."

Several adults in white coats reached up. They helped Priya and Yin out of the vent as well.

As her feet hit the carpet, Yin let out a deep breath. She looked up at the tunnel. Nothing moved in the black hole. She'd been so afraid. Maybe she had imagined the scraping sounds.

But they were safe now. They'd found help. She was glad that Sam hadn't listened to her.

"Er, thanks, Sam," Yin mumbled, unable to look her friend in the eye. "Looks like you saved us."

"Don't sound so shocked," Sam said. "I can be a pretty good leader too."

Yin felt her face grow hot. "I'm . . . I'm sorry if I made you feel like you weren't," she said.

Sam hugged Yin. She pulled Priya in for a group hug too.

"Look who else is here," Sam said as they pulled apart. She stepped aside, and Yin saw the three boys and the rest of their class – along with Brome.

Yin was astonished. "How?" she asked.

"We met Brome on our way out," said Mike. "He was coming back to the pod. We tried to find you, but you'd disappeared."

"I remember asking you to stay put," Brome said with a frown. Yin felt her face get hotter. She couldn't look at Brome either.

Ian handed Sam something pink. "I found some putty pieces on the floor when we searched for you. I thought you'd like them back."

Sam's mouth opened wide.

"But where's the rest?" Yin asked. "That's only a little bit of putty."

Ian shrugged. "It's all we found. We didn't see any on the walls."

Yin looked at Sam, who looked at Priya.

"The Monster Cabbage!" Sam shouted. Some of the ISS 3 crew looked over. "I bet it ate my putty. And it ate a whole person too!" She told the class and the crew about the lab and finding the foot. Everyone gasped.

"And we think that Calathea is . . . dead," Priya added. She shuddered.

An older woman in a lab coat covered her mouth. "Oh no! That poor girl!" she said.

The woman sank into the chair behind her. A man in a security uniform placed his hand on her shoulder.

"Except the Star Cabbage couldn't have hurt Calathea. That's impossible," Yin said. She put her hand into her pocket. The piece of plant was still there, and it hadn't moved at all.

"You're right," the woman in the lab coat said. "I'm Dr Anisol. I study the Star Cabbage, and it's harmless. It has nothing to do with this lockdown."

Yin started to tell her friends, "I told you." But she bit her lip instead.

"Then what *is* out there?" Sam asked.

Dr Anisol and the man in the security uniform looked at each other. Dr Anisol nodded. "Show them, Yuri," she said.

Yuri pulled a piece of paper out of his pocket. Everyone gathered around.

"This is the problem," Yuri said. "We call it Valeg."

Yuri held up a diagram of a terrifying creature. It looked like an experiment gone horribly wrong. The hulking cat-beast had spots like a leopard and two sets of stubby horns growing from its head. A ridge of spiky orange fur stood up all the way down its back. Long claws stabbed out of its huge paws and ended in points as sharp as knives.

Scariest of all were its eyes. They were two glowing yellow points – like laser beams ready to cut into their next victim.

"Where did it come from?" Yin asked. She couldn't stop staring at the picture.

Dr Anisol sighed. "As you know, we found the Star Cabbage on an asteroid," she said. "But that wasn't all. We didn't tell the public that we also found Valeg. At first, we only took the plants, but they died within days. The plants and Valeg need each other to survive. So we brought it onto the station too."

"Earth's leaders know about Valeg, but there are some groups that would be against keeping an alien creature like this," Yuri said. "They'd want us to destroy it."

"So we studied Valeg in secret," Dr Anisol added. "Valeg and the plants have such a unique relationship. It's like nothing we've ever seen."

"Well, your secret is out now," Yin said. "Valeg is roaming the station."

Yuri scowled. "We know. We've been trying to catch it for the past few hours. It's already wrecked the station's electrical systems."

"But how did Valeg even get free in the first place?" Priya asked.

Dr Anisol shook her head. "I think someone opened its cage. There's no way it could've escaped on its own."

"Well, however it happened, that group, Earth First?" Yuri said, rubbing his bald head. "They've been making so much trouble because of the Star Cabbage. And that's just a plant! Earth First is going to be furious when they find out a live alien creature is on the loose."

"Earth First?" Yin repeated. Slowly, something dawned on her. "That's where I know Calathea from! I knew she looked familiar!"

"What are you talking about?" Sam asked.

"That Holo-vid you showed us, Sam, back at the station," Yin said. "I didn't pay much attention to it, but I remember the person giving the speech at the protest. I thought she looked really young. It was Calathea! She's a member of Earth First."

"So, are you saying Calathea let Valeg out of its cage?" Yuri said.

Yin shrugged. "It's possible."

"And the girl was killed by her own silly plan,"
Dr Anisol said with a sigh. She turned to Yuri.
"Valeg may still be near that lab. It would make
sense it'd look for the plants it depends upon."

Yin secretly rubbed the plant piece in her
pocket. *Would Valeg come looking for my plant too?*
she thought. *Can the creature sense that it's here?*

Yuri called over a group of security officers
who were standing by a metal cage. The cage
had special technology that made it hover just
above the ground so it was easy to move – even
if it held a heavy alien creature like Valeg.

The officers listened as the three friends
described the lab where Calathea had been hiding.

"Don't worry," Yuri told the girls when they
had finished. "We'll find Valeg."

Just as he finished his sentence, a loud
metallic screech ripped through the canteen.

People screamed and rushed to the far wall. Yin and her friends turned in horror as a fierce cat-like head poked out of the hole in the ceiling – the same hole the girls had fallen through minutes before.

"It was right behind us!" Sam screamed, clutching onto Yin.

Long, deadly claws grabbed the edge of the vent hole. Muscular legs shivered as the creature perched above the room filled with its prey.

The glowing yellow eyes met Yin's. Her mind went blank. Her legs felt cemented to the floor.

Then the cat-beast pushed itself through the hole. It landed on a table with a soft, padded thud.

Valeg, the alien monster, had found them.

9

"Cage! Rods at the ready!" Yuri's voice boomed above everyone's screams. "Let's go!"

Yin felt Sam pull her away as the security officers pushed the hovering cage forward. They took out long metal rods from their belts. The ends crackled with blue light.

The creature jumped to the floor and let out a low growl.

"Don't hurt it!" Dr Anisol pleaded. She started to step forward, but Yuri held her back.

The security officers came closer. Valeg kept growling.

"It's OK, Valeg," Dr Anisol said quietly.

Valeg stopped growling and looked at the scientist. It blinked. Dr Anisol whispered something to Yuri, and he nodded.

Yuri let go of Dr Anisol's arm and walked by her side as she moved towards Valeg. She kept speaking in soft tones.

"You're safe, Valeg," Dr Anisol said.

The creature seemed to calm down at her voice, but the security team kept their rods raised.

Dr Anisol pulled a clear bag out of her pocket. Inside was a Star Cabbage. When Valeg saw it, a sound like a whimper came out of its fearsome mouth. The plant seemed to recognize Valeg too. It flapped back and forth.

Dr Anisol carefully placed the bag inside the open cage. Slowly, Valeg took a step closer. It took another step.

Then the creature pounced into the cage, tore the bag and slurped up the Star Cabbage. Valeg lay down inside the cage, quiet and happy.

The security officers slid the cage door shut. The other people in the canteen all let out a sigh of relief and applauded nervously.

Yin stared at the creature. She was more curious than scared now. As her friends joined the rest of the class, she edged closer to Valeg.

"So, it was hungry?" Yin asked the scientist.

"I don't think it eats the Star Cabbage the way we think of eating," Dr Anisol said. "The plants seem to affect Valeg's mood, almost as if they're talking to it. Their relationship is so different from any life on Earth."

Yin stood next to Dr Anisol and watched the alien creature sleep. "Valeg seems so small and harmless now," Yin whispered, not wanting to interrupt its slumber.

But another noise did. The main door to the canteen squealed open.

"Earth First will never let you keep that monster!" a voice shouted.

A panicked Calathea stood in the doorway. Her hair was sticking up in every direction. Deep purple circles lined her wide eyes. She was wearing a spacesuit now. And in her hand, she held a rod of her own. Its tip sparked with energy.

"She's alive!" Sam shrieked.

"She has a weapon!" Yuri yelled.

"No!" Dr Anisol cried. She stood between the cage and Calathea. "I won't let you hurt Valeg."

Yin found herself taking a stand right next to Dr Anisol.

"First you wasted money on the plants," Calathea said. Her eyes flicked from Dr Anisol to Yin and back. "Then you started playing with alien monsters! You're going to doom us all!"

Calathea rushed forward, shoving Dr Anisol and Yin to the side. She grabbed Valeg's cage and rolled it away. The security officers started to move towards her, but she swung the crackling rod at them.

Before anyone could stop her, Calathea had taken Valeg out of the room and slammed the canteen door shut. There was a metallic clanging outside, and then silence.

"Where is she taking Valeg?" Dr Anisol cried.

"I think she's going to kill it," Yin said. She was surprised that she felt sorry for the creature.

"Get the door open!" Yuri said. His team sprang into action. Calathea had blocked it somehow. It took several minutes before they slid the door open and rushed out into the corridor.

Yin ran after them.

"Where are you going?" Brome yelled. "Come back here!"

Yin ignored him. She had to see this to the end. And deep inside, part of her was actually worried about Valeg. She ran down the corridor. Behind her, Sam and Priya were running too.

Yuri and the security team easily made their way through the station. They went down a corridor into the central core and stopped in front of a large, red door with giant windows. Above were the words AIR LOCK 1.

"What is this place?" Sam asked, panting.

"An air lock is a series of rooms with locking doors that lead out into space," Yin explained quickly. "It's how astronauts get out of the station for space walks."

"So, Calathea is putting Valeg back into space?" Sam asked. "Isn't that good? It's where it comes from."

"Valeg came from an asteroid that was part of a planet," Dr Anisol said, coming up behind them. "And without the plants, Valeg will die. We can't let Calathea release it like this."

"She also has some of the Star Cabbage plants with her," Yuri said. He was looking through the thick glass door. "Calathea must have been planning all this for a long time to do everything so quickly."

The security team was trying to open the air lock door. It wouldn't budge.

Yin and her friends moved in closer to see what was going on. Calathea had her helmet on now as she stood behind a second door of heavy glass. A blinking red bulb above meant the room was locked and preparing to open to space. Valeg was beside her, but he was almost sleepy looking. Pots of plants sat on top of his cage. The stems were waving gently.

When Calathea saw everyone at the air lock door, she started yelling. "I tried to tell you this monster was dangerous," she shouted. Her voice sounded slightly electronic as it came through the intercom. "And these plants? They're not actually plants. They're intelligent! They have feelings!"

Calathea was frantic. Yin noticed that she had red blotches all over her face. They looked like the scratches that Yin had on her hand from the plant – only worse. Calathea's scratches were deeper. And they were dripping with yellow pus.

Calathea began to cry. "Why didn't anyone believe me when I told them these . . . aliens were talking to me? Not through words, but through my feelings. They were messing with my mind."

"It's all right, Calathea," Dr Anisol said in the same calm voice she had used to speak to Valeg.

"No, it's not! When we're not paying attention, they'll eat us for dinner and take over our planet," Calathea shouted. "I'm doing this to save Earth, can't you see?"

Dr Anisol turned to the girls and whispered, "I need to focus on getting the door open. Talk to her. Keep her from hitting that green button on the wall."

Yin stepped towards the door. "Please, Calathea. Let Dr Anisol help you."

Calathea ignored Yin. She checked the locks on her helmet.

Priya gave it a try. "What about the shoe?"

That made Calathea turn around. "Shoe?"

"In the lab," Sam added. "What happened?"

Calathea's face went blank, as if she was remembering something. "When the lockdown began, I . . . I went into that lab," she said. "The door opened, and Valeg appeared out of nowhere. He barged right past me. One of the scientists was simply watering the Star Cabbages. This monster pounced and . . . ate him."

"Dr Lee?" Dr Anisol said, looking up from the door controls. "That's horrible!"

"I locked the lab and tried to trap it, but Valeg just burst through the door," Calathea continued. She laughed and cried at the same time. The sound made Yin shiver. "You can't trust either the plant or the animal! But *I* will protect humanity."

Without warning, Calathea used her elbow to hit the green button on the wall. The far-side door slid open, and Calathea, the plants and Valeg were instantly sucked outside.

Outside – where there was nothing but dark space.

"Earth first! Earth always!" Calathea screamed.

She floated away with Valeg and the plants into the darkness.

"She's doesn't have a cable connecting her to the station!" Yin yelled. "She'll get lost out there. She'll die!"

Yuri was already barking orders at his team. Two officers ran out of the room.

Dr Anisol slowly turned to Yin and the girls. She looked stunned.

"Don't worry," she said, talking more to herself than to them. "We have drones that can fly out and grab her. She should be back on the station soon, and then she'll be taken to Earth."

"But what about Valeg?" Yin asked.

"The drones will get it too," Dr Anisol said. "Valeg doesn't need to breathe, so it'll be fine as long we get it quickly."

Sam and Priya looked shaken, but relieved. As Dr Anisol led them away, Yin kept turning back to look at Calathea, Valeg and the plants. They were slowly drifting out into the blackness. She had that feeling again – as if she had forgotten something, but couldn't remember what.

Then, something nudged Yin. She put her hand in her pocket. Her plant piece. It was wriggling.

"It's all right," she whispered to the plant. "I won't let anything happen to you."

She stroked it, and the tip curled around her finger. As she pulled away, the hairs on the plant dug into her skin. Yin stared at the new scratch. She almost expected it to fill with pus, like Calathea's wounds. It didn't.

"Are you coming, Yin?" Sam called.

Yin slid her hand behind her back. "Yeah, I'm right behind you."

"Thank you for all your help," Dr Anisol said to the classmates.

She shook hands with every one of them as they re-entered the pod. Soon after the girls had returned to the canteen, the ISS 3 crew finished fixing the electrical systems. The station's communication systems were back online. The blue warning lights stopped blinking. The lockdown was officially over.

Dr Anisol laughed nervously. "You've certainly had more adventure than you signed up for."

"More than I ever want in my life," Sam said. Still, she managed a smile.

Priya was more serious with her goodbyes. "You really should put Valeg back where it came from. It's too dangerous to have a creature like that on the station."

"I promise to think about it very seriously," Dr Anisol said.

Yin was the first one to sit down in her yellow seat inside the pod. She kept her hand wrapped around the plant piece in her pocket. It was the size of her hand now.

She couldn't wait to get home and put her plant in the ground, so it would grow full and strong. She was determined to keep it safe.

The pod filled with excited chatter as kids got on, but Yin kept to herself. A strange feeling was spreading through her. She couldn't decide if she was tired . . . or if it was something else. As her friends took their seats, Yin noticed that Priya's ponytails were swishing too loudly. Sam's breath smelled like rotten onions. She tried not to gag.

When Brome happily announced they were leaving the ISS 3, Yin's anger grew.

"Ugh, Brome's voice is so annoying!" she said. "Can't he keep his mouth shut?"

Her friends stared at her. "What's up with you, Yin?" Sam asked.

"Nothing," Yin snapped.

"My parents won't believe what happened," Priya said. "They'll probably never let me out of the house again."

"Well, I did warn you all. I told you it was the unluckiest day of the year," Sam said with a smile.

"Be quiet, Sam," Yin mumbled.

Sam didn't hear her. She was busy talking with Priya. Now that they were headed back to Earth, Sam was quite cheerful.

Yin bit her lip. *What's the matter with me?* she thought.

She didn't understand why her chest felt tight, or why every word out of her friends' mouths made her want to scream. So she shut her eyes and let the vines in her pocket tickle her skin.

She didn't care if her parents never let her go on another field trip. She didn't care if Sam and Priya thought she was bossy, or if they never spoke to her again.

The plant slowly twisted around Yin's fingers and started climbing up her wrist and into her sleeve. She thought she heard something. It sounded like *thank you*. But when she opened her eyes, no one was talking to her.

Yin closed her eyes again, and another odd feeling came over her. It started as a tingle in her fingertips and crawled all the way to the top of her head and bottom of her toes. It made her feel good. It made her feel powerful, angry and strong.

But most of all, it made her hungry.

SPACE PODS

Going up? Way, way up? In the future, space pods might be one easy method for taking humans and cargo from Earth's surface to orbiting space stations and back again.

A long, tough cable would stretch from an anchor point on Earth to an object in space called a counterweight. The counterweight would hold up the cable and need to be at least 35,400 kilometres (22,000 miles) above our planet's surface! The most expensive part of travelling into space with rockets is buying the fuel. But the pod of a space lift wouldn't need fuel. It'd travel along the cable, powered by rechargeable electromagnetic motors.

The pods would reach speeds of hundreds of kilometres an hour. Even at that speed, the trip into space could take several days. Pods would need to be built to withstand being hit by small meteorites. They would also carry their own oxygen supply.

What if there was a storm on Earth? Would it rip the lift cable to shreds? Not if it was built on the equator. Scientists say the equator is a fairly storm-free area, and that no hurricanes have ever crossed it. But . . . there's a first time for everything!

GLOSSARY

air lock room between two airtight doors that you use to go between areas of different pressure

dock join two spacecrafts together in space

drone aircraft with no people aboard that is controlled remotely

exhibit display that includes objects and information to teach people about a certain subject

hologram special type of image that looks solid and real, but is created with laser light

lockdown emergency situation where people are not allowed to enter or leave an area

prey animal hunted by another animal for food

pus yellowish-white fluid that is made when the body or a wound becomes infected

space walk period of time during which an astronaut is in space to do work outside the spacecraft

ABOUT THE AUTHOR

Ailynn Collins was born in England and has lived all over the world. Her love of learning has earned her a law degree, Montessori teaching credentials and an MFA in writing for children from Hamline University. She wrote the Redworld series and enjoys creating new worlds and all kinds of aliens. When not writing, Collins likes to work with her four dogs in dog shows and competitions, or she stays at home to read, often reading several books at once. She lives near Washington, USA.

ABOUT THE ILLUSTRATOR

Juan Calle is a former biologist turned science illustrator. Early on in his illustration career, he worked on field guides of plants and animals native to his country of origin, Colombia. Now he owns and works in his art studio, LIBERUM DONUM, creating concept art, storyboards and his passion: comic books.

READ MORE SCARY
SPACE ADVENTURES!

ALIEN LOCKDOWN

HAUNTED PLANET

THE FINAL MISSION

A HOLE IN THE DOME